The Blinks Make Me Think

The Blinks Make Me Think

by
Chet Jawor

Illustrations by
Micaela Jawor

DORRANCE
PUBLISHING CO
EST. 1920
PITTSBURGH, PENNSYLVANIA 15238

Dorrance Publishing Co
585 Alpha Drive
Suite 103
Pittsburgh, PA 15238
Visit our website at *www.dorrancebookstore.com*

ISBN: 978-1-4809-4493-0
eISBN: 978-1-4809-4470-1

Special credit and thanks to Julie, Danielle and Micaela for making the Blinks a very special story.

The Blinks
Make Me
Think

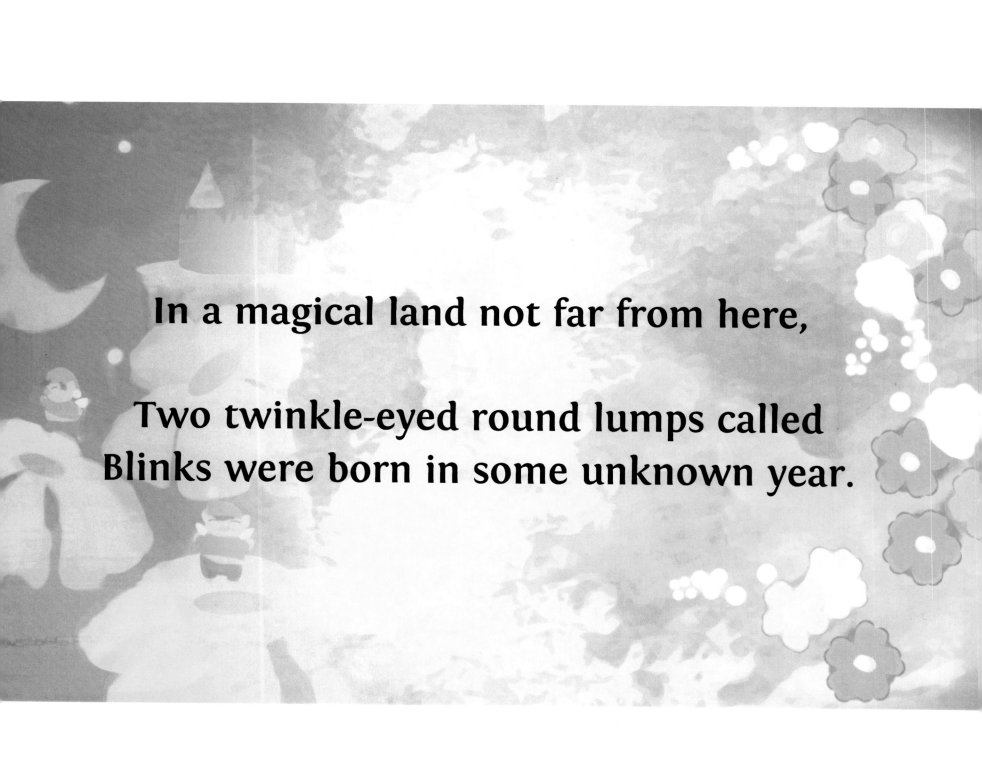

In a magical land not far from here,

Two twinkle-eyed round lumps called Blinks were born in some unknown year.

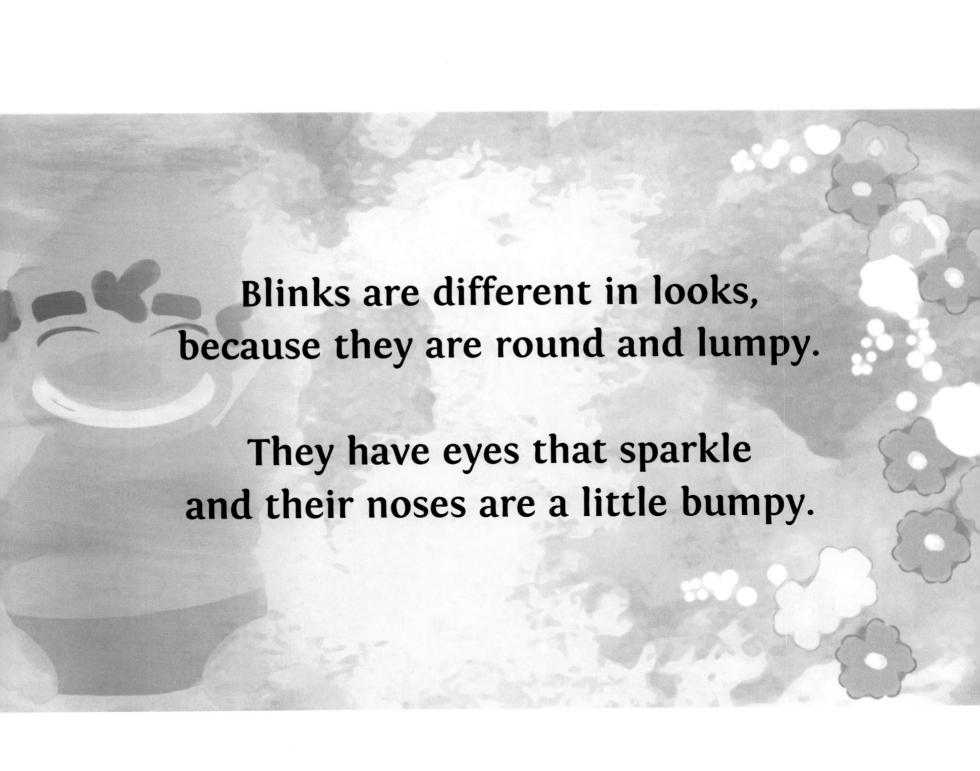

Blinks are different in looks,
because they are round and lumpy.

They have eyes that sparkle
and their noses are a little bumpy.

These Blinks are magical
and love to take flight.

They travel to your parents'
shoulders, both day and night.

They carry a magic that allows them to
show up here, there
and anywhere they need to be.

I once saw them in my room,
and soon after they were up in a tree.

They are quite like faeries
in some magical way.

They protect all children,
whether they sleep or play.

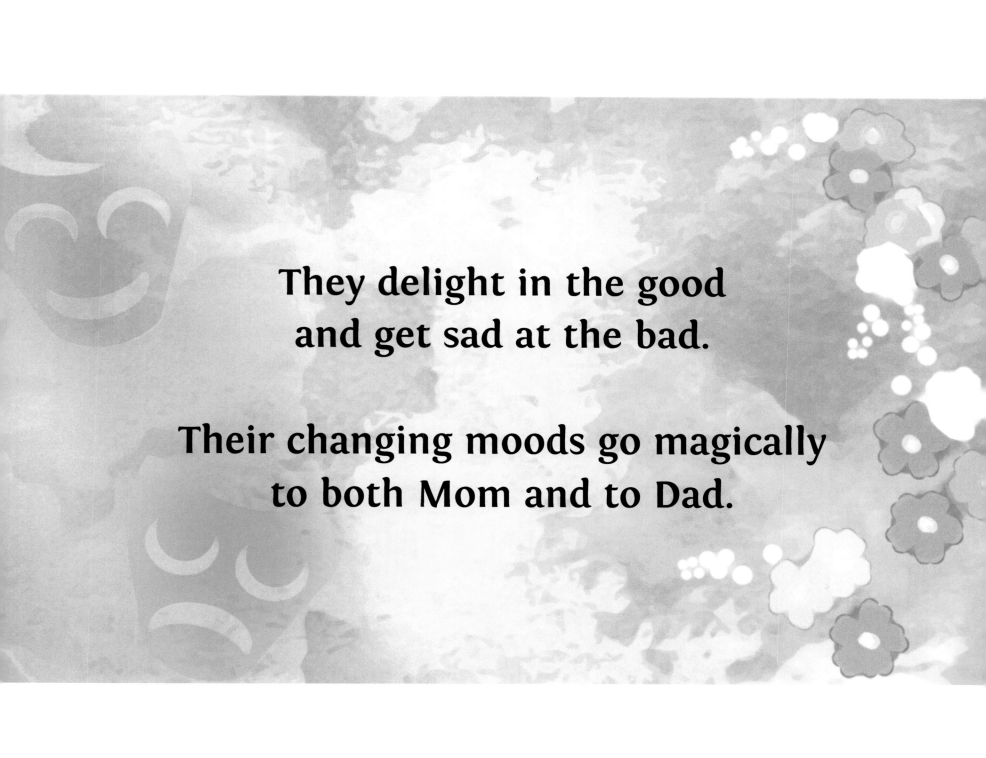

They delight in the good
and get sad at the bad.

Their changing moods go magically
to both Mom and to Dad.

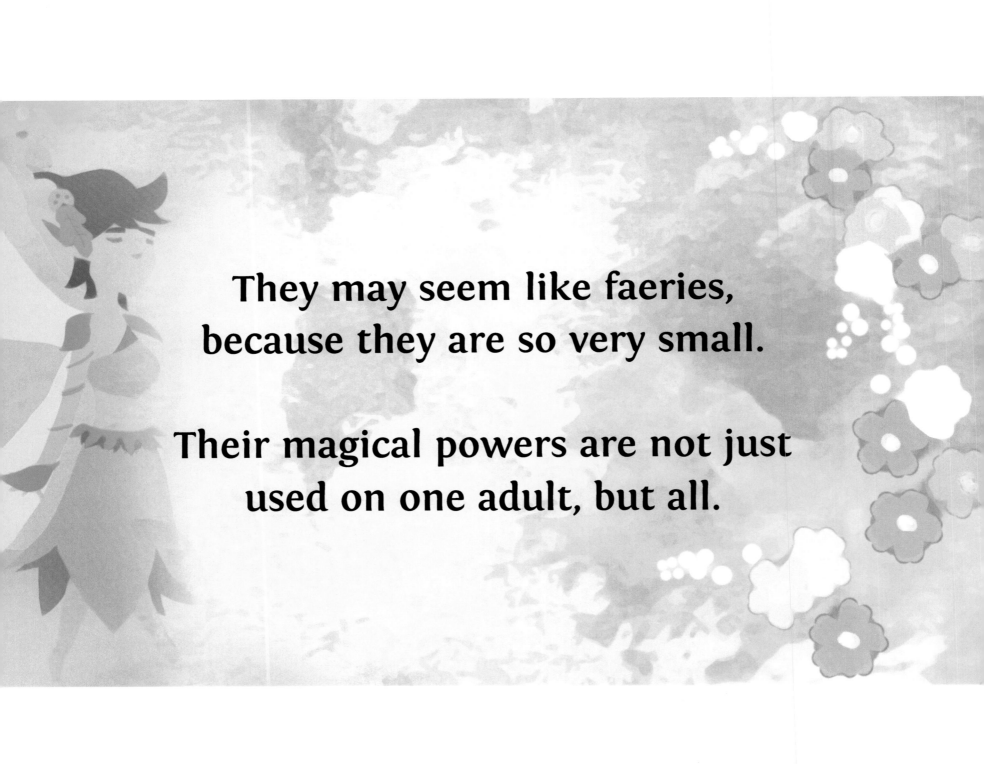

They may seem like faeries,
because they are so very small.

Their magical powers are not just
used on one adult, but all.

Now, let us be clear so we are not wrong.

Their magic works only on adults,
as they make sure their children are getting along.

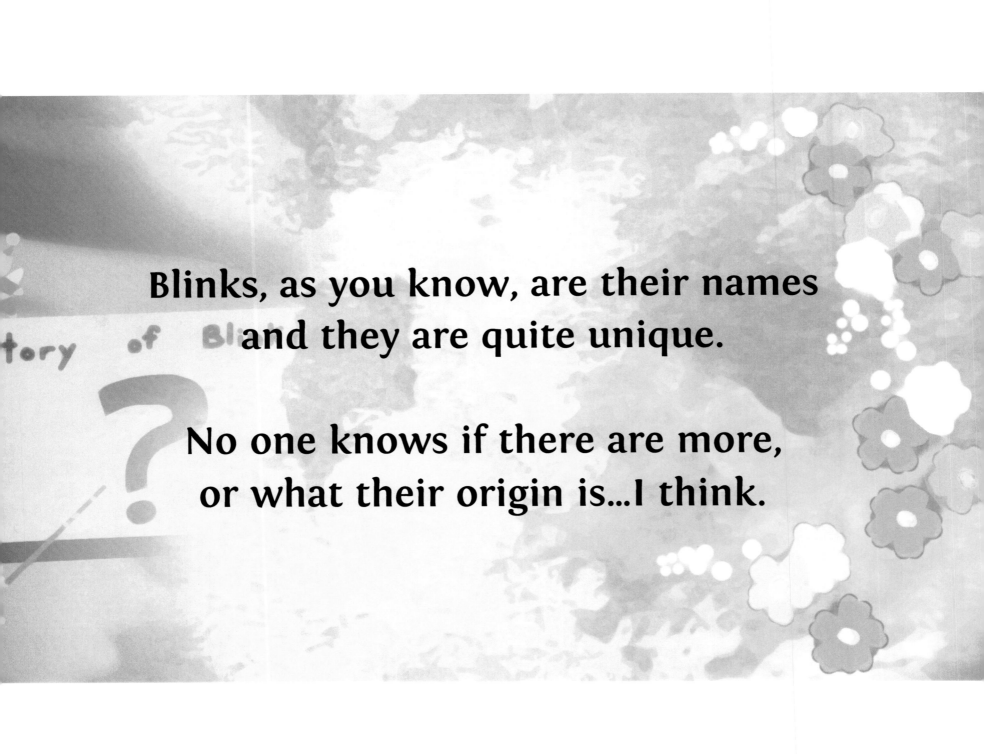

If a child misbehaves, a Stinky Blink
on an adult's shoulder, may appear.

However, if a child is good
then a Winky Blink might land
next to a guardian's ear.

When a child is causing trouble
for another girl or boy,

a Stinky Blink may appear
on an adult's shoulder
and pinch their ear to take away their joy.

The magical mood of a Stinky Blink
might make an adult get angry,
since the child did not behave
in a well-mannered way.

Well...the child may get sent to bed early
that very same day!

If a child is kind, then the adult and the child will laugh, smile, and play,

while the Winky Blink
keeps the Stinky Blink away.

Remember, if a child forgets to be good,
then the Stinky Blink will come
and cause sadness and tears.

But, just like before, the bad and the sad
can be changed to smiles and cheers.

All bad behaved children can always say
They're sorry to whoever they make sad.

So, learn to spread kindness to everyone
and the Winky Blinks will help you
to be happy and glad.

So, now as you close your eyes and dream say, "Goodnight," to Stinky and Winky Blink.

When you wake say, "Thank you, for helping me be good and making me think!"